good-bye for today

Good-bye for today

The Diary of a Young Girl at Sea

written by Peter and Connie Roop

❦

pictures by Thomas B. Allen

ATHENEUM BOOKS FOR YOUNG READERS

The authors would especially like to thank these courteous and helpful staffs for the "whale of a good job" they did in helping us with our research: the New Bedford Whaling Museum (particular thanks to Virginia Adams), New Bedford, MA; the Nantucket Whaling Museum, Nantucket, MA; Mystic Seaport, Mystic, CT; the Cape Cod Whalewatchers Boats, Cape Cod, MA; and The Whaling Museum, Lahaina, HI. We would also like to acknowledge the Dukes County Historical Society, Edgartown, MA, for the help they provided Peter Hanson in locating Laura Jernegan's diary.

Atheneum Books for Young Readers
An imprint of Simon & Schuster Children's Publishing Division
1230 Avenue of the Americas
New York, New York 10020
Text copyright © 2000 by Peter and Connie Roop
Illustrations copyright © 2000 by Thomas Allen
All rights reserved including the right of reproduction in whole or in part in any form.
Book design by Angela Carlino
The text of this book is set in Golden Cockerel ITC.
The illustrations are rendered in color pencils and oil wash. The small sketches are rendered in sepia ink with a bamboo pen.
Printed in Hong Kong
2 4 6 8 10 9 7 5 3 1
Library of Congress Cataloging-in-Publication Data
Roop, Peter.
Good-bye for today / by Peter and Connie Roop ; illustrated by Thomas Allen.
p.   cm.
Summary: Nine-year-old Laura writes in her journal about the boredom, excitement, and danger that she and her family face while sailing from Japan to the Arctic seas aboard the whaling ship captained by her father.
ISBN 0-689-82222-7 (alk. paper)
[1. Sea stories. 2. Whaling—Fiction. 3. Diaries—Fiction.]
I. Roop, Connie. II. Allen, Thomas B., ill. III. Title
PZ7.R6723Go 2000
[Fic]—dc21
99-27034   CIP

FIRST
EDITION

For Peter Hanson: May our voyage together continue!
P. R. and C. R.

To all the young sisters of the sea
T. A.

Glossary

AURORA BOREALIS: the Northern Lights; dim, brilliant streamers and bands of light seen in northern skies at night

BOW: the front part of a ship

BULL: male whale

CALICO: a coarse cloth with brightly printed patterns

CROW'S NEST: a small lookout platform near the tip of the ship's mast

DAGUERREOTYPE: an early photographic process in which the image is made on a light-sensitive silver-coated metal plate

FIRST MATE: a ship's officer, ranking just below the captain

FORECASTLE: the space near the bow of the ship where the sailors sleep and eat

JIBE: to shift a sail from one side of a vessel to the other while sailing before the wind

KEEL: the backbone of a ship; the wooden beam that runs from bow to stern at the bottom of a ship

ROMAN CANDLE: a firework which shoots up glowing balls

SANDWICH ISLANDS: the group of islands now called Hawaii. Named by the British explorer Captain James Cook in 1778

SECOND MATE: the next officer in rank after the first mate

SPY GLASS: a telescope

TACKS: the turns a sailboat makes to change direction

TAINTED: spoiled, rotten

WEEVILS: a kind of beetle

April 11, 1871

I do not want to write this journal. But Mama says I must. She tells me describing my life on the *Monticello* will make me a better writer. I don't want to be a better writer. I want to be a better artist. I'd rather draw pictures of what I see and do.

 My brother, William, doesn't have to keep a journal just because he is two years younger than me. I turned nine yesterday. Now I have to write a journal. It is part of my schooling. This journal was a present from Mama and Papa. I would have rather had new watercolors. Mine are getting old.

My name is Laura. I don't have anything else to say, so

Good-bye for today!

April 12, 1871

Mama says I must write in my journal every day like Papa does. Papa writes in his logbook each evening, but he has to as he is the captain. He writes about the wind and weather and what ships and whales we see.

When we chase whales, I'm sure that many things will happen. But mostly now my life is boring. Today we are anchored in Japan. The men are getting the ship ready to sail to the Arctic whaling grounds. Papa will hunt bowheads. I have never seen a bowhead. I

have seen sperm whales and humpbacks. I love it when the
humpbacks spout. Sometimes, when
the sun hits it just right, their spouts
look like rainbows. Here is my
picture of a humpback spouting
rainbows.

I don't have anything else to write, so

Good-bye for today

April 13, 1871

Papa ordered William and me to keep out of his way today.
When Papa gives an order, everyone obeys. *Immediately*. He is the
captain. The *Monticello* will be ready to sail tomorrow. We are
trapped like rats down belowdecks. Speaking of rats, I heard
one last night scratching beneath my bed. We need a cat to
catch the rats. Mama says *absolutely not*. No pets. Papa showed
me his logbook. He writes in it every day. I will try.

We had roast pork and potatoes for dinner.

Good-bye for today

April 14, 1871

We sailed from Japan. Papa says we will be gone for seven months
or until we fill every barrel on board. That's 2,600 barrels! I have
not sailed with Papa since I was three. Mama, William, and I have
lived on the Sandwich Islands since I was born in 1862.

We are sailing with Papa now because, after the barrels are all full, we are going home to New Bedford. I don't think of New Bedford as my home because I have never lived there. Honolulu is my home. But Mama and Papa grew up in New Bedford and that is home to them. I will get to see my grandparents for the first time. They are Papa's parents. I know what they look like because I have a daguerreotype of them. Mama's parents died before I got to meet them.

Good-bye for today

April 15, 1871

Mama gave me a Japanese doll for my birthday. I forgot to write about her. I named her Atsumi. She has black hair and wears a kimono. Here is my picture of Atsumi.

The *Monticello* looks nice. We have new sails and ropes. The sailors wear new silk headbands. Our cabin has been painted and smells nice. But I already miss the smell of flowers on shore. Atsumi smells like Japan when I hug her tight.

We sailed out of sight of land today. The ocean is so vast. *Vast* is my new word for today. Mama says I must find a new word each day, write what it means, learn to spell it, and use it in a sentence.

Vast means huge. *Vast* means very great. *Vast* means too many days to write in my journal, so

Good-bye for today

April 16, 1871

I worked on my lessons this morning. Papa built a schoolroom for us on deck. Mama is our teacher. I sit at one end of the table and William at the other. Mama is strict during schooltime. William gets in trouble with his mischief, like spilling ink on purpose.

I wonder what a real school is like with lots of children, not just a little brother? I have never been to school because there were no schools for girls in Honolulu.

Papa says this is my last voyage. Next year I will go to a proper school for young ladies. I wonder if proper young ladies know how to tie sailor's knots like I do.

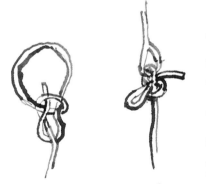

I don't want to go to school on land. I will miss Mama and Papa too much when they go whaling again. I might even miss William, but I doubt it. Atsumi is watching me write this. Maybe we will share our adventures with the proper young ladies.

Proper is today's new word. Mama says *proper* means correct behavior. Papa says it means shipshape. I like Papa's meaning best.

We had corn bread, beans, and pudding for supper. I used proper manners. William did not, so he got a whipping. He deserved it.

I did not think I could write so much, so

Good-bye for today

April 17, 1871

It rained today. All day. Thunder crashed like the waves. Lightning zigzagged across the sky. It rained so hard, water leaked down the hatch and soaked my journal. I was happy until Mama dried it by the cook's stove. Now these pages are all crinkly. William and I stayed belowdecks.

We have four ducks, three chickens, and one goat in a pen on deck. We get milk from the goat. We brought one of the ducks to our cabin to play with. I call her Lulu, after Honolulu, where I was born. She quacks and waddles and is funny. I begged Mama to let me keep Lulu as a pet. Mama likes Lulu but she said she had to talk to Papa.

He said, "No! Ducks are for roasting!"

Mean is my new word for today. *Mean* is stingy, greedy. Papa is so mean!

Good-bye for today

April 18, 1871

William is so lucky he is a boy! I wish I were a boy! Why? Because William got to swim today. I wanted to, but Mama said proper young ladies don't swim, even though I learned on the beach in Honolulu.

Papa tied a long rope to William. We were sailing slowly because there wasn't much wind. William jumped into the ocean and we pulled him along. He was laughing and having so much fun.

Cook made us duff for dessert today.

Duff is my new word. *Duff* is a flour pudding boiled in a bag. John Francis, the ship's cook, makes the best duff. I don't think proper young ladies eat duff, so I didn't eat mine, even though I love the raisins in it.

Good-bye for today

April 19, 1871

The day is sunny. We have not seen any whales or other ships, so I do not have much to write about. I will share my day.

My family shares the captain's cabin. It is not nearly so big as our home in Honolulu. Everything has a place and is in its place. There are four beds, two on each side of the cabin. The beds are built into the ship's walls. I like to put my ear against the wall and hear the ocean swish beside me. Drawers are built beneath the beds so we have a place for our clothes.

In the center of the cabin is Papa's table. That's where he looks at his maps and where we eat our meals. At the back of the cabin is Mama's sofa. She refused to sail with Papa without it. I like to lie on it and read or talk with Mama when she sews, or watch Papa write in his logbook. If we see a ship he lets William stamp it in the book. I will get to stamp the whales. (If we ever see any!) The stamps are wooden blocks Papa has carved. Instead of drawing a new picture each time we see a ship or a whale, he stamps it. I would rather draw it myself. Maybe Papa will let me do that. It would make his logbook look ever so much nicer.

Each morning after we rise, either William or I have to empty the chamber pot over the ship's side. We hate this job! Our washroom is tiny, but better than what the sailors use. In it we have a washbasin and a toilet. The toilet is a wooden seat with the  chamber pot beneath it. I wonder if proper young ladies have to empty their own chamber pots?

After breakfast we have school, and the day fills up with other things.

My arm aches from writing so much, so

Good-bye for today

April 20, 1871

We saw sharks today! William and I climbed on the railing at the stern and watched the sharks following the ship. I wonder if the proper young ladies have ever seen a shark?

Ben Merry, a boat steerer, harpooned one and pulled it on deck. It flipped around trying to bite him until he hit it with a club. Ben gave William and me one of the teeth. It is very sharp. I would hate to fall in the water when sharks are nearby! And I certainly would not want to swim. Here is my picture of the shark.

We had shark steaks for dinner. Cook made shark stew for the crew.

Boat steerer is my new word. The boat steerer is the man who steers a whaleboat. Sometimes he is the man who harpoons the whales, too. Ben Merry is a fine boat steerer. He is also my favorite sailor of all twenty on board. He wants us to call him by his nickname, "B. Merry," but Mama will not allow it, as it is not proper. There is that word again!

Good-bye for today

April 26, 1871

I have not written for a long time as I have been sick. For days I lay in bed holding Atsumi. I had a terrible fever. Now I feel ever so much better.

The wind was strong all day. Papa said we made 160 miles since yesterday, the most so far. Still, it is a long way to the Arctic.

Mama started to teach us geography today. I learned about Africa. Maybe someday we can sail there. Papa says only if there are whales. Papa showed me where we are on his sailing chart.

Chart is my new word. A chart is a map of the land and ocean. Papa buys charts and makes his own, too.

Papa says when I am completely well he will build a swing for us. That will be fun.

Good-bye for today

May 1, 1871

Papa built us the swing. It hangs from one of the booms. At first I was scared to climb on it, but after I learned how, I played on it all afternoon.

I finished my third reader today, too. It is colder today. Papa says it will get colder each day as we sail north.

Mama is already unpacking our woolen clothes. She says we will need them before long. Living in Honolulu I was never really cold before.

In my geography book there is a picture of a person called an Eskimo. They live in the Arctic. I wonder if we will see any? *Eskimo* is my new word.

Good-bye for today

May 2, 1871

The ship is going fast. We have a very strong wind pushing us. Papa thinks a storm is building in the distance.

Something funny happened today. Mama is always telling William to be careful near the railings. When the weather is calm, he likes to walk on them when she isn't looking.

Today the cook threw a bucket of rotten potatoes overboard. Mama thought William had fallen in the ocean. When she learned what really happened, she did not laugh at first, but later she did.

Cook made beef and potatoes for supper. I think we will be eating lots of potatoes because one barrel is spoiling.

No new word, so

Good-bye for today

May 3, 1871

Today Papa took me by myself in one of the whaling boats. He showed me how to set the sails. He taught me how to jibe and come about and how to run with the wind. He even let me steer.

The ocean is so vast in the small boat. I hope Papa and I get to sail again soon.

William is so jealous because Papa said he was too young to sail. I like being older. William said girls couldn't sail. Papa told him about Mrs. Mayhew from Cape Cod. Like Mama, she sailed with her husband and family. Her husband died near the coast of Africa. Mrs. Mayhew navigated the ship around Africa and across the Atlantic to home.

Papa called her a "sister of the sea." I like being a girl. I like being a "sister of the sea." I wonder if proper young ladies are ever sisters of the sea?

Navigate is my new word. *Navigate,* means to find your way from one place to another on the sea. Papa navigates using the sun during the day and stars at night. His charts help us know where we are. I hope we never get lost. Or Papa gets sick. I could not navigate us home like Mrs. Mayhew. Neither could Mama. These thoughts frighten me, so

Good-bye for today

May 10, 1871

I have not written for a long time. Today is a sad day. Jim Walker, a sailor, was washed overboard. Papa just read the service for Mr. Walker's soul. I am sad, because I have never known anyone who died.

This is what happened. I am glad now I am writing a journal, for I never wish to forget this dreadful time.

Papa was right about the storm. First it was far away. We could see the wind whipping up the waves to the west. Papa ordered the sailors to batten the hatches and tie down everything loose.

"We are in for a blow," he whispered to Mama, but I overheard. It is hard to keep secrets on a small ship. "You must keep Laura and William secure below."

I wanted to stay on deck. But I knew better than to argue with Papa. He was worried about the ship and us.

Below in our cabin we heard the wind whistle through the rigging. It howled so loudly I covered my ears. The waves were like mountains. The *Monticello* leaped through the waves like a galloping horse. We rode up and up on the front of the waves and slid down the back. We could only look out our tiny porthole at

the terrible seas. The waves were capped with white froth. Here is my picture of the waves.

We put anything loose in our chest and in the drawers under the beds. Still, things wrenched loose and slid back and forth across the cabin. Mama ordered us into our beds. I hung on by digging my fingernails into the wood of my bed.

Waves broke over the ship. We heard the water rushing across the deck. Water ran down the hatches, dripping on our beds and our clothes chest. Mama tried to stop the leaks but there were too many.

Mama kept looking at the door as if she wanted to go up on deck with Papa. I wondered how he fared. Later I learned that Papa had been lashed to the wheel so he would not get swept away in the waves. Papa is too brave for words.

All of the sailors on deck had ropes tied to their waists to keep them from getting washed overboard. Papa told me poor Jim Walker's rope snapped when one particularly monstrous wave hit us. The wave carried him so fast that no one could grab him before he went overboard. The wind was too strong for Papa to turn back to look for him. This is too horrible to write about anymore.

We tossed for hours. We were cold and damp. William complained about being hungry. Mama explained that Cook could not light the stove because the ship rolled so much. I did not care, for my stomach was heaving. I wonder if proper young ladies ever throw up? I bet they would have during the storm.

The storm blew all day and night. Once, when I dozed, I almost fell from my bed. Mama climbed in bed with William and held him, he whimpered so. Will he ever grow up to be as brave as Papa? I wanted to join them but I was too grown-up.

Finally the storm blew itself out. Papa called the storm a typhoon. I call it a horrible, terrible monster that I never want to see again. Papa says we might have more. I pray we do not. For the first time I look forward to being on dry land, at school with the proper young ladies.

Good-bye for today

May 15, 1871

There has not been anything to write about. Every day is the same. We sail and we sail. We see ocean. And more ocean. We do our lessons in the morning and play in the afternoon. William sits and watches the sailors do their jobs: sharpening harpoons and knives, mending sails, washing their clothes, scrubbing the deck, splicing rope, repairing ratlines.

I have been helping Mama make a quilt. She calls it her log cabin quilt. I trim the pieces before she sews them into a large blanket. Lulu took Atsumi when I wasn't

looking and hid her. I finally found her in Lulu's nest. I think Lulu
is going to lay eggs. That is good news. If she says lots of eggs, then
Papa won't roast her. She is my pet even if Papa doesn't think so.

I have no new word, so

Good-bye for today

May 17, 1871

We saw land far away. It was a mountain with snow on the top. Papa
says we are almost to where the whales are. It is very cold now.
Mama is making me a new dress for boarding school. I am making
Atsumi a dress from the scraps to keep her warm. She looks very
pretty. I wonder when we will see ice. Papa says we won't see
icebergs like in my geography book. The ice where we are going will
be flat, and huge rafts of it drift about. He says it can be very
dangerous there because the ice can surround a ship and crush it.
But he told me not to worry. He would make sure that didn't
happen. Still, one sailor told me he was on a ship that the ice caught,
and he escaped with only the clothes he was wearing. If the ice ever
traps us, I will rescue Atsumi first, then Lulu! We had green peas and
hardtack for dinner. The weevils are in the hardtack. We tap them
on the table until the bugs fall out, then we dip the hardtack in
water to soften them. I wonder if they serve hardtack and peas at the
boarding school? I wonder if proper young ladies know how to get
weevils out of hardtack? If they don't, I'll show them.

Good-bye for today

May 30, 1871

Even with the wind the water is flat as a pancake. I like it. It feels different from when the ship is rolling on the open ocean. We must be closer to shore. The men made the ship ready for the ice. They took down the highest sails because we won't need them. They hammered copper onto the bow to push the ice away. They put up the crow's nest. I want to go up in the crow's nest, but Papa will not let me. He says maybe when it is not windy. I hope it is calm tomorrow. Mr. Hall, the second mate, hung out his wash to dry, but it froze. I am in the fourth reader. Although I am only nine years old, Mama says I will be in fifth grade when I go to boarding school. I wonder what it is like to go to school on land? Papa is very busy now. We had duck eggs for supper. William ate four!

Good-bye for today

June 3, 1871

Last night I got very scared. A loud scratching noise awoke me. It sounded like long fingers scraping the ship's sides. William laughed at me when I told him. It was only ice he said. I think he was scared, or why was he awake, too?

It was ice. The most ice I have ever seen! It was everywhere—in front of us, behind us, all around us. Some pieces were as big as the *Monticello*. Others were the size of beds. The small pieces were like skillets. It was so bright my eyes hurt. Papa let me look at the ice with his spyglass. I was scared. Papa said this ice wouldn't hurt us. It was too broken apart. The bad ice is the giant rafts that push a ship against the shore and crush it into matchsticks. It is so cold I want Lulu to sleep with me. Mama says *absolutely not!* We had baked potatoes for supper.

Good-bye for today

June 18, 1871

Papa let me go up in the crow's nest. I saw a whale! At first it looked like the ocean was bubbling. Then all at once a great black back pushed up out of the water. The whale spouted and made noises. It sounded like *pahhhhhhhhhhhhhhhhhhhh*. Papa was with me, and he let me shout, "Thar she blows!" The men went after the

 whale, but it got away by diving under the ice. Papa was angry, but I was glad. I didn't want my first whale to be cut up and boiled for oil.

Good-bye for today

June 25, 1871

Fog. Fog. Fog. Nothing but fog for five days. It was like being inside a gray blanket. Mama made me lie in my bed all afternoon because I was so grumpy. Atsumi doesn't like the fog either. I told her the story of Beauty and the Beast. I fell asleep. William cut himself with a sailor's knife. He was trying to carve a picture on a whale's tooth like Isaac does. Mama bandaged it. He says it still hurts. We had pancakes for supper. They were good.

Good-bye for today

June 27, 1871

It is a good thing Mama knows how to sew so well, because she had to sew a sailor's ear back on today. Somehow, Tom Leek cut his ear off while sharpening his harpoon. It was bleeding frightfully. Papa brought poor Tom into our cabin. Tom handed Mama his bloody ear and she stitched it back on just like she was stitching her quilt. Did Mama learn how to do that at boarding school? I doubt it.

Good-bye for today

June 29, 1871

It is quite pleasant today. We saw six whales. Papa lowered the boats and the chase was on. I watched through Papa's spyglass. Isaac was the boat steerer in one boat, and Mr. Hall in the other. I watched Isaac's boat the most. The men rowed as hard as they could after the whale. Part of me wanted them catch it and part of me wanted it to escape. When they got near the whale,

Tom Leek stood up and balanced on the bow with his harpoon ready. All at once he threw his harpoon. The harpoon struck the whale. The whale flapped its flukes and dived. The rope snaked out until there wasn't any left. Then the whale started pulling the boat faster and faster up and over the waves. The men call this a "Nantucket sleigh ride." Finally the whale tired and the men came close and killed it. I was sad, but Papa says we have to hunt the whales or starve. The men waited in their boat with their whale until we sailed up close to them. Then they cut a hole in a fluke and towed the whale next to the ship. Mr. Hall's boat also got a whale.

Isaac's whale is as long as the ship. The men are cutting it in right now. Papa said they would get both whales cut in tonight, but I think they will only get one. William is up on deck watching the men cut off the blubber. I wish I could go watch, too, but Mama says it is not for

young ladies. I wish I were an old lady, then. Why does William get to do everything just because he is a boy? I will ask Papa if I can watch the next whale. Mama is reading a book. I will draw a picture of a whale now, just like Papa does in his log book. Here is my whale.

Good-bye for today

June 30, 1871

Papa said I could watch them cut in the second whale. Mama was not happy! When they cut off the blubber it looks like they are peeling a giant orange. The strips of blubber are hauled up on deck and dropped into the blubber room. There the men cut the blubber into thin pieces called "Bible leaves." Then the men boil out the blubber in try-pots. The pots are real large. Before the men boil out the blubber, they get in the pots and squeeze out the blubber and are up to their knees in oil. The whales smell dreadful. Isaac's whale made seventy-five barrels of oil. That will light a great many lanterns! The whalebone was stacked along the rails to be cleaned later. Papa gave me a piece of whalebone. It is hard but bends easily. Mama says it is good for making umbrellas, fishing poles, whip handles, and policemen's clubs. When the men finished, they washed off the deck. It smells much better. The men are very happy. They know each whale means they will share $10,000.

When the men finished, they shouted, "Hurrah, hurrah! Five and forty more!" That means good luck for the next hunt.

Good-bye for today

July 1, 1871

It is a pleasant day. It is quite smooth. There is more ice than ever.

Good-bye for today

July 2, 1871

When someone spots a whale, Papa gives him five pounds of tobacco. It is almost supper time and I can't think of much to

write. I went to bed last night and got up this morning. We will have baked potatoes and biscuits for supper. Would you like to hear some news? Well, I don't know of any.

Good-bye for today

July 4, 1871

Independence Day. Happy Fourth of July! Papa let the men have the day off. He took me sailing again. I love sailing with just Papa. We swish through the water like a whale. Today I sailed most of the time. Papa relaxed, but I know he was always watching me just in case a sudden gust of wind caught us. We would freeze to death in the water before the *Monticello* caught up to us. Mama is displeased when I sail with Papa, I am not. It is something special just we two share. William is so jealous! Papa says he can learn to sail when he is older. Today I like being the oldest again.

Isaac made a Roman candle with gunpowder. It looked so pretty when it blasted off into the night sky. Papa let William shoot some Chinese firecrackers he bought in Japan. They were so loud Lulu hid. I told Atsumi about Independence Day because in Japan they don't have it. Papa says we have 460 barrels of oil now. Cook made an Independence Day treat for us: corn bread with molasses, coconut, and beans.

Good-bye for today

July 10, 1871

Last night the sky was on fire! It was like the Independence Day fireworks, but better. Green, yellow, violet, and orange streamers danced across the sky. Sometimes the lights hung like curtains. Then they would change and become towers. They would dip down and shoot up. Mama called them the northern lights. My geography book says they are the aurora borealis. Isaac told me the Eskimos are scared of them. They think the lights will harm them. I asked why, but no one knows. Mama said we are only guests here. It is like the Eskimos not understanding why we kill whales but don't eat them. I wonder if we will see any Eskimos?

Good-bye for today

July 11, 12, 13, and 14, 1871

Wind, water, weather, whales.

Good-bye for today

July 21, 1871

Papa exchanged messages with the ship *Emily Morgan*. Later, Captain and Mrs. Dexter came on board for a gam. *Gam* is my word for today. It's when people from different boats visit one another. It was fun! Mrs. Dexter had news of New Bedford that we had not heard. Mama had a long list of questions to ask. I have never been to New Bedford, but it must be pretty. I hope my grandma is nice like Mrs. Dexter. We gave them five duck eggs, some sweet potatoes, lime juice, and a few pumpkins. They gave us calico, some coconuts, and a pig. Papa and Captain Dexter talked about whales and weather the whole time. We had the pig for supper. We will have bacon tomorrow morning!

Good-bye for today

August 2, 1871

This is the coldest day so far. The sun is bright but not warm. The water is calm. It is ever so busy on board and I find little time to write. The men took another whale. William said it would be fifty barrels of oil. I guessed sixty. I was right. We ate the last of the pig today. My hands are too cold to write any more, another reason to keep these entries short.

Good-bye for today

August 4, 1871

Papa let William go with Isaac to hunt walrus today. He almost got killed! I was watching through Papa's spyglass. Isaac and his crew got close to an ice raft with five walrus on it. One old bull with tusks like daggers got angry and dived into the water. It swam straight at the boat. I shouted, but they didn't hear me. The walrus dug his tusks into the boat and pulled out a plank.

William said the tusk almost stabbed his leg. The men killed the walrus. Isaac cut off its tusks and gave one to William. Isaac is going to carve a picture of the walrus attacking William on it.
William wanted to put his tusk under his pillow. Mama said, *absolutely not* until it is perfectly clean.

Good-bye for today

August 7, 1871

The men took two whales today. Hustle and bustle everywhere. There are many other whaling ships here. Papa says Captain Frazier told him there are more than thirty. I can see smoke from six ships trying out blubber. I hope they don't take all of the whales. Papa will be unhappy. We had corn bread and beans for supper.

Good-bye for today

August 10, 1871

Lulu blew overboard today! The wind was so strong it blew her into the water. She couldn't fly back up because Mama had clipped her wings. Papa had a boat lowered to fetch her, but she had frozen to death before they got her. Atsumi and I cried ourselves to sleep. William is upset just because now he can't have any more duck eggs. He's heartless and mean.

Good-bye for today

August 12, 1871

There is more ice than before. Papa spends all day on deck. Two men are always in the crow's nest looking for ways through the ice. Papa says it is like sailing through a maze. We had pancakes for supper. I miss Lulu!

Good-bye for today

August 14, 1871

Four Eskimos came on board. They paddled to us in their sealskin boats. They wear pieces of ivory in holes in their cheeks. One kept looking at Atsumi. I let him hold her. He smiled and rocked her like a baby. I wonder if he has a little girl? Does she have a doll? Papa talked with the Eskimos. He knows some words because he has been here before. The Eskimos told him they have never seen so much ice. The wind keeps pushing the ice up close to shore, not far out like it usually does. They said winter will be here early this season. Papa gave them sharp knives to thank them. I wonder if the proper young ladies have ever seen an Eskimo? Here is my picture of their boat.

Good-bye for today

August 17, 1871

The wind was very strong. We almost sank. Papa took us through a channel in the ice, but the ice moved. We were sailing very fast and hit the ice. The ship tilted on its side and made a most horrible noise. I was on deck and held on to the railing as hard as I could. When the ship tilted I was looking straight up at the sky. We slipped off the ice and crashed into more ice. We went way up on the ice and then slid off backward. Papa told the men to man the pumps, but even after hitting ice twice, we had no holes. Mama says we were very lucky. She asked Papa if we shouldn't turn back. Papa said no, we still don't have enough oil. Atsumi stays in my bed now. It is too dangerous for her on deck. We had sweet potatoes for supper.

Good-bye for today

August 20, 1871

Isaac finished carving William's walrus tusk. The walrus is attacking the boat, ready to stab his tusks into William. Papa says it is the best scrimshaw he has seen. *Scrimshaw* is my word for today. It is what they call the pictures cut into the ivory and stained with ink. William follows Isaac around and acts like him now. Mama lets William sleep with the tusk under his pillow. Here is my picture of William's tusk.

Good-bye for today

August 23, 1871

Papa is happy again. A strong wind from the east blew the ice away from us. Now there are ten miles of open water. Papa said we can sail up to Point Barrow where we will find plenty of whales. The men are happy, too. They did not want to leave yet either. Mama is still worried. She and Papa talked quietly together. Mama frowned. We had beans for supper.

Good-bye for today

August 25, 1871

The men took three whales. Papa said we will add almost two hundred more barrels of oil. He says he made the right decision to stay. The men are so busy cutting in that they let another whale go. I wonder if it was my whale?

Good-bye for today

August 27, 1871

Today is a sad day. One of the sailors, Peter Pennybacker, had been ill for some time. He had the most terrible cough. Even after all that Mama could do for him, he died. We buried him at sea this afternoon. The entire crew gathered to say "fare thee well." Poor Peter was wrapped in a piece of sailcloth. After we said prayers for his soul he was confined to the deep. It seemed so cruel to bury him so far from home, but there is no way to carry his body back to New Bedford. Papa auctioned off his belongings. That seemed cruel, too, until Papa explained that the money would go to his widow. I feel sad for her. Her husband has died and she will not know it for at least another year when we arrive in New Bedford. Will my husband be a whaler like Papa? I know now why Mama insisted that we sail to New Bedford with Papa.

Good-bye for today

August 29, 1871

A terrible, frustrating day! The wind is strong. It snowed so hard that we could barely see anything. We were off Point Belcher. The ice was moving back our way. Papa turned the ship around. The ice was so close we had to tack many times. We went a few miles, but it was very shallow. We were just ready to tack again, when a great raft of ice slid under our bow. We struck the ice and stuck.  The men lowered the sails and put out anchors. We slipped off the ice, but then we stuck on the bottom. Papa hopes we don't have to abandon the ship. He will decide tomorrow. Papa and Mama talked a long time.

Good-bye for today

August 30, 1871

What a surprise in the morning! Other ships were all around us. The water was calm and many sailors rowed over to help us. It was like a gala party! More anchors were put out. Casks of oil were hauled up and loaded on the stern. After much scraping against the bottom the *Monticello* floated again! The other ships towed us off and we dropped anchor between the ice and the shore. Papa is smiling again. Cook made duff to celebrate. I ate every bit of mine!

Good-bye for today

September 1, 1871

Papa sent the boats out looking for whales. The weather was pleasant. Everyone prayed and whistled for a strong wind to blow the ice farther away. The wind didn't come. The ice did. It drifted closer and closer. We had beans and bread for supper. I don't think I have ever been this cold before. How I wish for the warmth of the Sandwich Islands. Is it this cold in New Bedford?

Good-bye for today

September 2, 1871

I am so scared I can hardly write this. Three ships sank yesterday. The ice crushed the *Comet*. The *Roman* was trapped and squeezed. When the ice moved away, the *Roman* had so many leaks she sank. The *Awashonks* was pushed up on the ice and her keel cracked. No one was hurt, but Papa says they lost five hundred barrels of oil. Papa is worried now when he looks at the sky and the ice. He is going to meet with the other captains on the *Florida* tomorrow. Together they will discuss when it is too dangerous to stay.

Good-bye for today

September 8, 1871

We have not moved for a week. The ice comes in and goes out but not far enough for us to escape. We watch it fearfully. There is nothing we can do. William told me the men say we are probably going to abandon the ship. I don't think so. Mama finished her quilt. It is beautiful. She will let me sleep under it tonight. I will be really warm!

Good-bye for today

September 9, 1871

The captains met again. Seven ships got free of the ice. They will wait for us as long as they can. Ice is all around us except for a small strip by the shore. Mama began packing a chest of warm clothes. Papa says she worries too much. But I could tell he is worried, too. I think Mama is right. I helped her pack.

Good-bye for today

September 12, 1871

All the captains met last night. We will abandon the ships in two days! Papa says we cannot take anything except food, clothing, and blankets. William must leave his tusk behind. I begged Papa to let me take Atsumi. He said no. Atsumi and I cried ourselves to sleep. Papa is so mean. I will throw this journal overboard if I cannot take Atsumi.

Good-bye for today

September 13, 1871

The men were busy all day fixing the whaleboats and getting ready to leave. Papa inspected everything to be loaded. I held Atsumi all day. I did not talk to Papa. Mama cried when he said she couldn't take her china dishes. She bought them last year and they are her favorites. Papa says she can take her quilt. Tomorrow we leave.

Good-bye for today

September 14, 1871

The wind is blowing hard. I cannot sleep. We are by a big fire on land. Mama says I can write in my journal. She took it from the ship and tucked it in her blouse. I never had a chance to throw it overboard. We left the *Monticello* this morning. It was sad. Papa had a hurt look in his eyes I have never seen before. We walked  around the ship one last time. Our cabin looked just like we were coming back. Mama insisted we make the beds. William sniffled a lot when he put his tusk under his pillow. I tucked Atsumi under the covers. I cried. Mama held me. Papa was the last one out of the cabin. We raised the flag upside down. That means the ship is abandoned. We sailed all day in a whaleboat. We got wet and very cold. Papa never looked back at the *Monticello*. Dozens of other whaleboats bobbed along with us. Everyone is trying to escape the ice. Now we are camping on a rocky beach. We have three big fires. It is snowing now. The snow is making the ink run. My hands are freezing. I want Atsumi!

Good-bye for today

September 15, 1871

Today we almost died. This is what happened. Papa was sailing the boat when a great gust hit the sail. The boom swung hard and fast. It smacked Papa in the head so hard he was knocked out. Mama held Papa and tried to wake him up. The sail flapped. A chunk of ice was moving right toward us. Neither Mama nor William know how to sail, so I grabbed the sheet and hauled it in. It took Papa a long time to wake up. When he saw me at the tiller, he smiled as if he had got five whales. He called me a "true sister of the sea." Can proper young ladies sail a whaleboat?

Good-bye for today

September 16, 1871

We are on board the *Progress*. It escaped the ice. When we climbed the rope ladder, William almost got washed away by a big wave. He is bragging about it now, but I know he was scared. It completely covered him! Papa says we will sail to Honolulu and take another ship to New Bedford. Then Papa surprised us. After dinner he held out his hands. William's tusk was in one and Atsumi was in the other! I hugged Papa so hard my arms hurt. I am so happy, I cannot sleep. But Mama says I must try. I am glad I kept this journal. I will share it with the proper young ladies. They won't believe it! Atsumi does. She was there.

Good-bye forever

Authors' Note:

Good-Bye for Today is based on two real whaling families: the Williamses and the Jernegans. In telling Laura's story we used the "voice" of Laura Jernegan, who sailed aboard the whaler *Roman*. Laura, as part of her education aboard the *Roman*, kept a journal which stills exists. At the end of each day's journal entry, Laura wrote "Good-Bye for Today." Mary Williams also sailed aboard a whaling ship with her family. We do not know if Mary kept a journal, but many of Laura's experiences in this book are based on the true adventures of Mary Williams. In our research we discovered that it is quite likely that Laura and Mary knew each other in Hawaii.

Many children were born and grew up on whaling ships, rarely setting foot on solid land. They went to school aboard the ship, learning their ABCs from their mothers, and whaling and sailing skills from their fathers and their crews. Whaling ships with a wife or family aboard were nicknamed "hen's frigates."

Life aboard a "hen's frigate" was not easy for a whaling family. Friends were few and far between. Whaling families ate the same food as the sailors: stale water; biscuits with weevils in them; salted beef; and once in while, fresh fruit and vegetables. The sickening stench of the "cutting in" and "trying out" coated their clothes. There were more rats than a ship's cat could take care of, and cockroaches, as whalers said, "with teeth so sharp they could eat the edge off a razor." The cockroaches, however, helped keep the fleas under control! Living space was small, cramped, and crowded. One sailor said, "The forecastle was black and slimy with filth, very small, and hot as an oven. It was filled with foul air, smoke, sea-chests, soap-kegs, greasy pans, and tainted meat." Even the captain had little space to spare on a ship wishing to leave as much room as possible for barrels of valuable oil.

For a whaling family, life was filled with adventure and danger. Terrible storms, in which a careless sailor could get washed overboard, had to be weathered. And there were the thrilling whale hunts, when you dropped everything at the shout of "Thar she blows!" and the chase was on. We hope this book will help others understand that American whaling was an industry and, while it brought many whale species close to extinction, our ancestors hunted whales for food, oil, and bone that they could not get any other way. Today these needs can, and must, be supplied by other sources, so the sea will always have its gentle giants and we can appreciate the whales for their beauty and grace.